# WINTER WOOD

# DAVID SPOHN
# WINTER

# WOOD

LOTHROP, LEE & SHEPARD BOOKS    NEW YORK

Copyright © 1991 by David Spohn
All rights reserved. No part of this book may be reproduced or utilized in any form or by any means,
electronic or mechanical, including photocopying and recording, or by any information storage
and retrieval system, without permission in writing from the Publisher. Inquiries should be
addressed to Lothrop, Lee & Shepard Books, a division of William Morrow & Company, Inc.,
1350 Avenue of the Americas, New York, New York 10019. Printed in Italy by L.E.G.O.

First Edition   1   2   3   4   5   6   7   8   9   10

Library of Congress Cataloging in Publication Data
Spohn, David. Winter wood / by David Spohn.
p.     cm. Summary: A young boy and his father go out to the winter woods to chop firewood,
enjoying the work and the natural world around them.   ISBN 0-688-10093-7 — ISBN 0-688-10094-5
(lib. bdg.)   [1. Fuelwood cutting—Fiction.   2. Forests and forestry—Fiction.   3. Fathers and sons—
Fiction.]   I. Title.
PZ7.S7635Wi     1991     [Fic]—dc20
90-49944 CIP AC

to my grandpas

Outside the kitchen window, the thermometer says 10° below zero. Birds at the feeder fluff out their feathers in the morning sun.

Inside, Matt and his dad sit at the table and eat
their breakfast. It's Saturday morning, time to bring
in wood to keep the house warm.

After he has finished his oatmeal, Matt buttons up
his flannel shirt. Then he pulls on his snowpants
and his red wool sweater.

While Dad sips the last of his coffee, Matt puts on
his boots.

Then both zip up their jackets, pull their stocking hats down over their ears, and wrap their scarves around their necks.

They put on gloves and mittens, and they are off, down to the woodpile. Dad carries the axe over his shoulder. Matt pulls the sled behind him.

They get right to work, moving quickly to stay warm.
Dad brings the axe down and the wood pops open.
A pile of split logs begins to grow. Matt hurries to
load the pieces onto the sled.

Pretty soon another pile starts. Matt and his dad
are getting very warm. They untie their scarves and
throw them up on the woodpile.

Matt works hard to load the wood as fast as Dad splits it. Soon both of them are sweating. They unzip their jackets and throw them on the woodpile, too. It isn't long before they're tired.

"We need a break," says Dad.

They each sit down on a big log to rest for a while.

The air around them is crisp and still and has the smell of dry oak. They sit and talk about woodpile things, like how nicely the wood splits when it's so cold, and how the sound of steel into wood echoes through the air when you hit it just right. They watch the birds, now darting from tree to tree around them. Nuthatches, chickadees, and bluejays.

They laugh at their breath as it comes out in little clouds, then vanishes.

Then Dad finds a couple of small pieces of wood for
Matt to try.

Even though the axe is really too big for him, Matt wants to show his dad that he can split wood, too. He smiles with pride when the logs break open at his feet.

Then it's time to get back to work. Matt watches the axe circle through the air. A sharp crack and the wood splits in half. Matt loads it on the sled as Dad picks up another log.

The sun is nearing its highest winter reach.
"That's enough for now," says Dad.
They pick up tools and jackets and scarves and
head back to the house with the sled full of wood.

Matt leads the way. Dad, moving slower now, pulls the sled. By lunchtime the woodbox is full. The rest of the wood is stacked just outside the kitchen door.

As they load up the stove, Matt thinks he remembers each and every piece. Then Dad tells him again what Grandpa used to say:

"Winter wood warms you twice—once when you cut it...

and again when you burn it."